THE TALE OF
THE FLOPSY BUNNIES

BY BEATRIX POTTER

FREDERICK WARNE

IT is said that the effect of eating too much lettuce is "soporific".

I have never felt sleepy after eating lettuces; but then *I* am not a rabbit.

They certainly had a very soporific effect upon the Flopsy Bunnies!

FOR ALL LITTLE FRIENDS OF

MR. McGREGOR & PETER & BENJAMIN

FREDERICK WARNE

Published by the Penguin Group
Registered office: 80 Strand, London, WC2R 0RL
Penguin Young Readers Group, 345 Hudson Street, New York, N.Y. 10014, USA

First published 1909 by Frederick Warne
This edition with new reproductions of Beatrix Potter's book illustrations first published 2006
This edition copyright © Frederick Warne & Co. 2006
Reissued 2016
New reproductions of Beatrix Potter's book illustrations copyright © Frederick Warne & Co. 2002
Original copyright in text and illustrations © Frederick Warne & Co., 1909

Frederick Warne & Co. is the owner of all rights, copyrights and trademarks
in the Beatrix Potter character names and illustrations.

Manufactured in China

Special Markets ISBN 978-0-723-26018-9

WHEN Benjamin Bunny grew up, he married his Cousin Flopsy. They had a large family, and they were very improvident and cheerful.

I do not remember the separate names of their children; they were generally called the "Flopsy Bunnies".

AS there was not always quite enough to eat –
Benjamin used to borrow cabbages from Flopsy's
brother, Peter Rabbit, who kept a nursery garden.

SOMETIMES
Peter Rabbit had
no cabbages to
spare.

When this
happened, the
Flopsy Bunnies
went across the
field to a rubbish
heap, in the
ditch outside
Mr. McGregor's
garden.

MR. McGregor's rubbish heap was a mixture. There were jam pots and paper bags, and mountains of chopped grass from the mowing machine (which always tasted oily), and some rotten vegetable marrows and an old boot or two. One day—oh joy!—there were a quantity of overgrown lettuces, which had "shot" into flower.

THE Flopsy Bunnies simply stuffed lettuces.
By degrees, one after another, they were overcome
with slumber, and lay down in the mown grass.
  Benjamin was not so much overcome as his
children. Before going to sleep he was sufficiently
wide awake to put a paper bag over his head to
keep off the flies.

THE little Flopsy Bunnies slept delightfully in the warm sun. From the lawn beyond the garden came the distant clacketty sound of the mowing machine. The bluebottles buzzed about the wall, and a little old mouse picked over the rubbish among the jam pots.

(I can tell you her name, she was called Thomasina Tittlemouse, a wood-mouse with a long tail.)

SHE rustled across the paper bag, and awakened Benjamin Bunny.

The mouse apologized profusely, and said that she knew Peter Rabbit.

WHILE she and Benjamin were talking, close under the wall, they heard a heavy tread above their heads; and suddenly Mr. McGregor emptied out a sackful of lawn mowings right upon the top of the sleeping Flopsy Bunnies! Benjamin shrank down under his paper bag. The mouse hid in a jam pot.

THE little rabbits smiled sweetly in their sleep under the shower of grass; they did not awake because the lettuces had been so soporific.

They dreamt that their mother Flopsy was tucking them up in a hay bed.

Mr. McGregor looked down after emptying his sack. He saw some funny little brown tips of ears sticking up through the lawn mowings. He stared at them for some time.

PRESENTLY a fly settled on one of them and it moved.

Mr. McGregor climbed down on to the rubbish heap—

"One, two, three, four! five! six leetle rabbits!" said he as he dropped them into his sack.

The Flopsy Bunnies dreamt that their mother was turning them over in bed. They stirred a little in their sleep, but still they did not wake up.

Mr. McGregor tied up the sack and left it on the wall.

He went to put away the mowing machine.

WHILE he was gone, Mrs. Flopsy Bunny (who had remained at home) came across the field.
  She looked suspiciously at the sack and wondered where everybody was?

THEN the mouse came out of her jam pot, and
Benjamin took the paper bag off his head, and they
told the doleful tale.

Benjamin and Flopsy were in despair, they could
not undo the string.

But Mrs. Tittlemouse was a resourceful person.
She nibbled a hole in the bottom corner of
the sack.

THE little rabbits were pulled out and pinched
to wake them.

Their parents stuffed the empty sack with three
rotten vegetable marrows, an old blacking-brush
and two decayed turnips.

THEN they all hid under a bush and watched for Mr. McGregor.

Mr. McGregor came back and picked up the sack, and carried it off.

He carried it hanging down, as if it were rather heavy.

The Flopsy Bunnies followed at a safe distance.

THEY watched him go into his house.
And then they crept up to the window to listen.

MR. McGREGOR threw down the sack on the stone floor in a way that would have been extremely painful to the Flopsy Bunnies, if they had happened to have been inside it.

They could hear him drag his chair on the flags, and chuckle—

"One, two, three, four, five, six leetle rabbits!" said Mr. McGregor.

"EH? What's that? What have they been spoiling now?" enquired Mrs. McGregor.

"One, two, three, four, five, six leetle fat rabbits!" repeated Mr. McGregor, counting on his fingers— "one, two, three—"

"Don't you be silly; what do you mean, you silly old man?"

"In the sack! one, two, three, four, five, six!" replied Mr. McGregor.

(The youngest Flopsy Bunny got upon the window-sill.)

MRS. McGREGOR took hold of the sack and felt it. She said she could feel six, but they must be old rabbits, because they were so hard and all different shapes.

"Not fit to eat; but the skins will do fine to line my old cloak."

"Line your old cloak?" shouted Mr. McGregor— "I shall sell them and buy myself baccy!"

"Rabbit tobacco! I shall skin them and cut off their heads."

MRS. McGREGOR untied the sack and put her hand inside.

When she felt the vegetables she became very very angry. She said that Mr. McGregor had "done it a purpose".

AND Mr. McGregor was very angry too.
One of the rotten marrows came flying through
the kitchen window, and hit the youngest
Flopsy Bunny.

It was rather hurt.

THEN Benjamin and Flopsy thought that it was time to go home.

SO Mr. McGregor did not get his tobacco, and
Mrs. McGregor did not get her rabbit skins.

But next Christmas Thomasina Tittlemouse got a
present of enough rabbit-wool to make herself
a cloak and a hood, and a handsome muff and a pair
of warm mittens.